To: Maddy
F
October 2001

Happy Birthday to You!

By

Marianne Richmond

Happy Birthday to You!

is dedicated to
the deserving birthday boy or girl
in all of us. — MR

LCCN: 2007903348

Marianne Richmond Studios, Inc.
3900 Stinson Boulevard NE
Minneapolis, MN 55421
www.mariannerichmond.com

ISBN 10: 1-934082-09-0
ISBN 13: 978-1-934082-09-6

Illustrations by Marianne Richmond

Book design by Sara Dare Biscan

Printed in China

First Printing

Also available from author & illustrator
Marianne Richmond:

The Gift of an Angel
The Gift of a Memory
Hooray for You!
The Gifts of being Grand
I Love You So...
Dear Daughter
Dear Son
Dear Granddaughter
Dear Grandson
My Shoes take me Where I Want to Go
Fish Kisses and Gorilla Hugs

Plus, she offers the *simply said...* and *smartly said...* mini book titles for all occasions.

To learn more about Marianne's products,

please visit

www.mariannerichmond.com

Happy Birthday to You!

By
Marianne Richmond

Open your eyes!
Get ready to play...
From morning 'til night,
this is your day!

day to you!

What will you do?
What fun will you plan?
What memories will make
your birthday grand?

with chocolate milk, of course, or soda pop instead!"

Dance in your pajamas.
Sing a silly song.

Bring cookies to your neighbors.
Smile all day long!

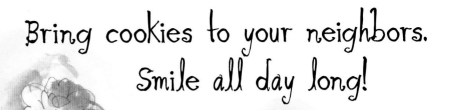

Buy yourself some flowers.
Throw confetti while you walk.

Decorate your driveway with multi-colored chalk!

"A party would be fabulous,"
you say, "for two or ten or twenty.

Would it be okay if I hoped for presents plenty?"

PresenTS HERE

KARAOKE

Hope for all you want today.
Wish for dreams come true.
No one is more deserving
than fantastic, awesome you!

Choose your favorite clothes
and wear 'em all together.
Parade around the town
no matter what the weather.

Blow up red 'n orange balloons
and launch them to and fro,
brightening up the sky above
for your birthday down below.

"I'll do a kartwheel in my kitchen
    for every year of me."
Then you say, "I think I may
            go on a chocolate spree!"

Fill your 'tum' with tasty treats
for no reason but because

you're the only you there is,
and that deserves applause!

"Do I look a little taller?"
You ask with proud delight.
"Is my brain a little smarter
since the mid of yesternight?

Another year taller!

Proportionate.

Stretching out.

Can ride the roller coaster!

Taller than Sheila and Marcy.

Your birthday is our chance to share our biggest cheer
for who you are inside
each day of **every** year.

Your feelings and ideas, your jokes and sweetest smile.
Your hugs and
kind affection.

Your
quirky,
perky
style.

We
Love You!

Count us one by one,
the circle of all those
who love you and adore you
from your head

down

to

your

toes.

"I think I need a rest," you say,
    "from all the lively fun,
to count my many blessings
    before the day is done...."

Not quite yet, you know,
    you still have more to do,
to share the joy and happiness
    of simply being you!

Spray your sis with silly string!

Give juggling
a try.

Find a kiddie
playground...

Swing and touch the sky!

Roll down the biggest hill
    and sprawl out afterward.
Feel the thrill of possibility
    in this big, wide open world.

Make a deal between yourself
    on the intro date of you,
to learn one something different
    and try another new.